DISNEY
Winnie the Pooh

The Essential Guide

honeybee

morning stretches

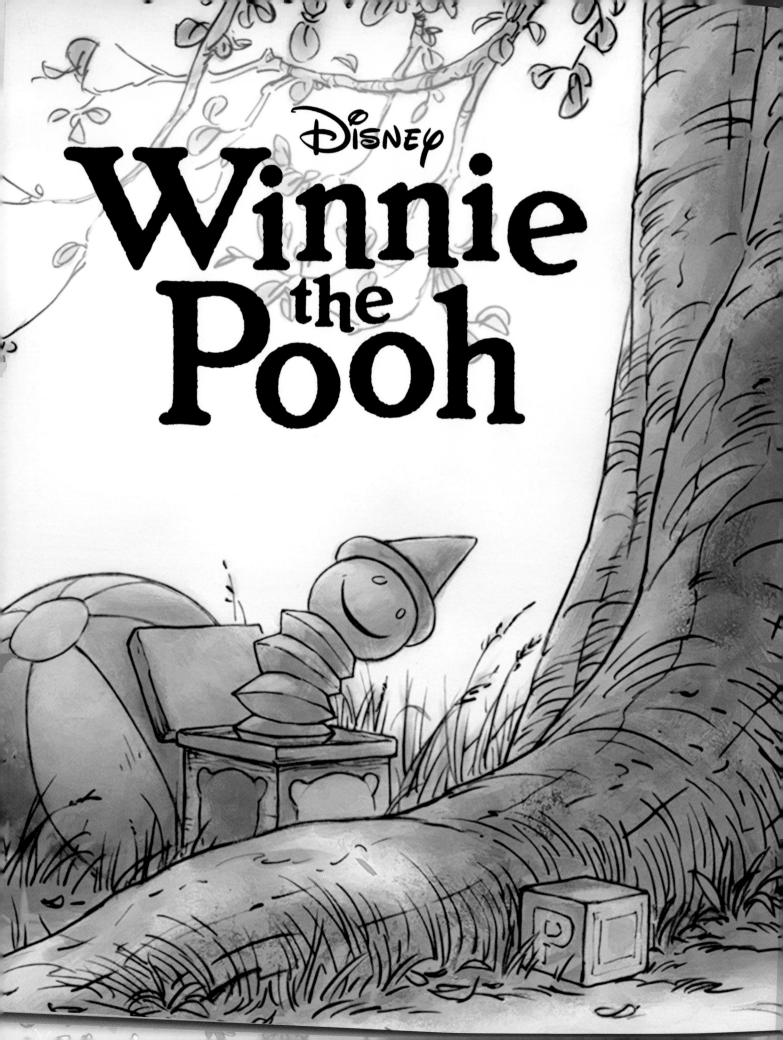

Contents

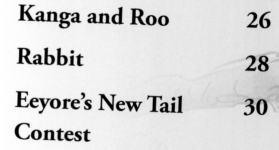

Introduction

Who is a chubby, fuzzy bear with very little brain, a big heart, and an enormous fondness for honey? It's Winnie the Pooh, of course! Pooh and his friends live in the Hundred-Acre Wood, where they spend their days happily exploring, adventuring, and looking for Important Things to Do. What sort of Important Things need to be done? Look inside to find out!

honeybee

Winnie the Pooh

A Pooh Bear's head may be filled with fluff, but as long as his tummy is filled with honey, he will never complain. After all, the most Important Things are being helpful and finding more honey!

bee

tummy

Honey Tummy
Pooh's roly-poly belly takes care to maintain. For his morning exercise, he reaches toward his toes, humming encouragingly to himself.

"Is that you, Tummy?"

honey

bee

Pooh's House

Pooh lives in a house in the Hundred-Acre Wood. If you ring or knock, he will answer very politely, and perhaps invite you in for elevenses.

Important things:

A pot of ooey, gooey honey is Winnie the Pooh's favorite treat.

Honeybees are a bear's best friend—but the bees might not feel the same way about Pooh!

Pooh so loves his friends that he will stop looking for honey when one of them needs a helping hand—or a tail.

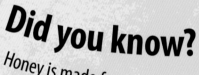

Did you know?

Honey is made from nectar and pollen that bees collect from flowers.

When his tummy rumbles, Winnie the Pooh listens. "What's that, tummy? Time for more honey?"

Best of Friends

Whether hatching a plan to find honey or digging a hole to catch a monster, every bear needs a big-hearted friend like Piglet.

Christopher Robin

rumpled hair

Christopher Robin is the best friend an animal could have. Everyone in the Hundred-Acre Wood looks up to him as a beloved leader. His friends trust his plans completely and follow him faithfully.

Close Friend

Christopher Robin is always nearby to lend a helping hand to a friend in trouble. His cheerful outlook fills his furry friends with hope.

"Silly ol' bear!"

Robin's Nest

A green door on the east end of the Wood marks the entrance to Christopher Robin's woodland home.

Bear and Boy

Every boy needs a bear like Winnie the Pooh to talk to, care for, and—from time to time—rescue.

Listen Up!

When Christopher Robin has something to say, his animal friends are eager to pay close attention. They do not always understand, but they do their very best to support their friend.

plant

Did you know?

Christopher Robin's favorite game is called "Pooh Sticks." It involves two people dropping sticks from a bridge into a river and seeing which stick travels quickest.

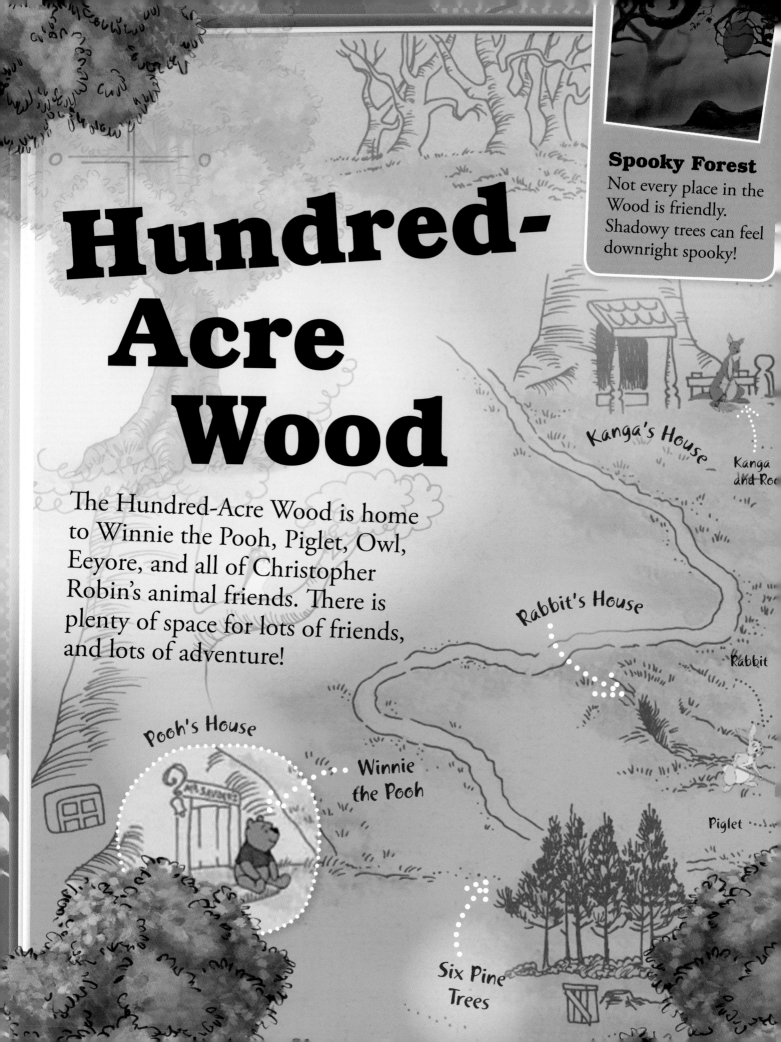

Hundred-Acre Wood

The Hundred-Acre Wood is home to Winnie the Pooh, Piglet, Owl, Eeyore, and all of Christopher Robin's animal friends. There is plenty of space for lots of friends, and lots of adventure!

Spooky Forest
Not every place in the Wood is friendly. Shadowy trees can feel downright spooky!

Kanga's House

Kanga and Roo

Rabbit's House

Rabbit

Pooh's House

Winnie the Pooh

Piglet

Six Pine Trees

Bee Tree
Winnie the Pooh's favorite kind of tree holds hives filled with honey. The bees like it, too!

B'loon

swing

Christopher Robin's House

Meeting Place
Between adventures, the friends have a special place to discuss Important Things and plan expeditions.

Eeyore's Gloomy Place

Owl's House

Eeyore

Pooh's House

Winnie the Pooh's home is just right for a Pooh Bear, with a cozy bed and a table set for breakfast. Do you want to look inside? Use the big knocker and "ring also" to tell Pooh you are there.

honey-colored flower

busy honeybee

A Sweet Spot
Pooh's favorite spot in his house to enjoy a pot of sticky honey is his comfortable armchair.

Pooh's Kitchen
A Pooh Bear takes care of his tummy, and that means he must make sure his kitchen is filled with honey.

Did you know?
Above Pooh's door is a sign that reads "Mr. Sanderz." Mr. Sanders lived there before Pooh did.

Helpful reminders:

Pooh's Pooh-koo clock helps him to remember when there is a Very Important Thing to be done.

Pooh's rumbly tummy reminds him when he needs more sweet honey to eat.

chimney

Pooh's Place

To find Pooh's house, walk across the Wood from Christopher Robin's house, over the river, and past six pine trees.

MR. SANDERS

RNIG ALSO

nice, wide door

window

Piglet

Piglet may be a Very Small Animal, but he plays a big role when there is a Very Important Thing to be done. It just goes to show, you do not have to be very big or very brave to be a very, very good friend.

twitchy ears

be

sweet smile

Little Piglet

Piglet owes his sweet smile to his modest, kind, helpful nature—and his faith that Christopher Robin can fix just about anything.

Best Buddies

Piglet and Pooh are devoted best friends. Together, they enjoy life's simple pleasures far more than weighty books or heavy thinking.

"The bees are quite gentle."

a lovely flower

Well Beehived

Piglet is always willing to help out his best friend. Even if that means going head first into a beehive to help Pooh find honey.

Oh D-D-D-Dear!

When you are Very Small, it is wise to be careful. Whenever he can, timid Piglet tries to steer himself—and honey-hunting Pooh—away from danger.

Here to Help

Everyone lends a hand—or a head—when there is a job to be done in the Hundred-Acre Wood, and no one works harder than Piglet!

Piglet's talents:

- Helping his friends.
- Tying a bow.
- Sitting on a bouncy jack-in-the-box.
- Writing "Piglit."
- Hopping into Kanga's pouch.
- Being very brave when his friends need him to be.

Did you know?

Piglet's favorite things to eat are acorns, or "haycorns." He planted one in his garden so it would grow into a useful supply of haycorns.

17

Eeyore

Even the brightest of days seem rather gloomy in Eeyore's corner of the Wood. And when things go wrong—which they usually do—how does an old gray donkey feel? Not very "how" at all.

Un-gloomy things:

 When nights are cold and snowy, there is no better shelter than a stick-house made by friends.

 A cheerful bow brightens up the back of Eeyore when his tail is nailed on tight.

 Snacking on spiky thistles gives a donkey something to do on lonely days.

Dour Donkey

A donkey is not the same without his tail. Not that life was so very sunny even with it, but still...

mane

floppy ears

18

B'loon

Prickly Pastime
Sometimes when a donkey does not know what to think, the only thing to do is munch on some thistles and wait for the next misfortune.

Oomph!
It is bad enough to lose a tail, but to lose your balance on the same morning? It can only be the start of an extra-gloomy day. Thank goodness for friends like Pooh.

"Something swingy perhaps?"

Did you know?
A thistle is a plant covered in thorny spikes. Most animals won't eat them, but donkeys will.

Home Sweet Home
Some might say it looks like a pile of sticks, but Eeyore's humble house provides a little warmth and comfort in his blustery corner of the Hundred-Acre Wood.

tasty thistle

19

Owl

If anyone knows anything about anything, it is Owl who knows something about something. He has a gift for writing—especially instructive signs and memoirs.

Book Owl

When something needs to be explained, whether it is biscuits, barnacles, or Backsons, Owl turns to his extensive library of books.

a long book

Listen Up

Everyone trusts Owl's knowledge of mysteries and monsters, which gives him a great deal of authority—and a flair for drama.

The Very Tree

Owl is writing his memoirs so he revisits important sites to tell the story of his life. First stop, for "Chapter 1: The Birth of a Genius" is the very tree where Owl was born.

Did you know?

Although Owl likes to think he is very knowledgable, he is not so good at spelling his name. He spells it "Wol."

notebook

The birth of a genius"

flapping wings

Owl's landmarks:

His birthplace: An enormous tree in the Wood, marked by a growth chart from Owl's earliest days.

The Chestnuts: Owl's old house, which was later knocked down in a storm.

The Wolery: An ideal new home for an educated owl. It was formerly Piglet's house.

fine feathers

The Thing to Do

Owl has a talent for telling others what to do—a useful service when one's friends have fluff instead of brains.

A Very Important Thing to Do

The Hundred-Acre Wood is a big place, so to spread Very Important news and call friends together, a sign is a good idea. The only thing better is LOTS of signs!

sign

garden fence

Christopher Robin's pencil

Written...
When something needs to be done, Christopher Robin can be counted on to get the point across: "A vary importnt thing to do!"

Posted...

When a message is Very Important, one can never have too many signs. Rabbit's garden is the perfect spot for the gang to plant lots of them.

pumpkin

And Found!

Could Rabbit's garden be growing signs instead of carrots? One thing is for sure—Rabbit doesn't look very happy about it!

Tigger

Tiggers are pouncy, flouncy, and friendly as can be. What they like best of all is to bounce. Nobody bounces quite like a Tigger! They would be very good at swimming and flying too, if only they wanted to.

Tiggerific Tail

Tigger's tail is as bouncy as a spring. It is what gives Tigger his bouncy, trouncy, flounciness!

A What?

Tigger makes a very good audience for anyone with a tale to tell. Do you know about an adventure? As long as the story is packed with action, he is all ears!

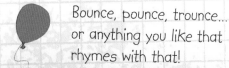

"...the most...wonderful thing...about Tiggers...

How to be a Tigger:

Bounce, pounce, trounce... or anything you like that rhymes with that!

Always be on the hunt for fun or on the tail of a terribly busy monster.

Be the only one.

Did you know?

Tigger likes to eat honey, haycorns, and thistles, but his favorite thing is Roo's special strengthening medicine: Extract of Malt.

Fun, Fun, Fun!
Even when life takes surprising turns, Tigger greets each new challenge—like a play-fight with B'loon—with boldness and good cheer.

springy tail

Undercover Tigger
If you can hear a rustle in the bushes and a growl that isn't Pooh's rumbly tummy, look out! It is probably an undercover Tigger preparing to pounce on you.

B'loon

...is that I'm.........the only one!"

springy spring

Kanga and...

Kind Kanga lives with her son, Roo, in the Hundred-Acre Wood. Roo may be a little bundle of energy, but Kanga never tires of caring for him with lots of love and hugs.

"Seems like someone...

Home from Home
Kanga keeps her home warm and welcoming for her darling little Roo.

Loving Mother
Gentle Kanga shares her motherly advice, encouraging smile, and soothing cuddles with all the animals in the Hundred-Acre Wood.

26

Perfect Fit

Tiny Roo fits perfectly in his mother's pouch. It is the ideal place to see the world while staying out of harm's way.

..could really use a hug!"

mailbox for two

sweater made by Kanga

...Roo

Happy Son

Cheerful Roo loves simple joys like bouncing high and playing with the bigger animals. He knows the safety of his mother's pouch is never far away!

Hopping hobbies:

Kanga spends her spare moments knitting soft scarves, cozy mittens, and warm earmuffs.

Roo prefers to fill his time drawing pictures using colorful crayons.

knitted earmuffs

Rabbit

Like Owl, Rabbit has actual brains between his ears—and he knows how to use them. If there is a plan to be made or a trap to be constructed, Rabbit is always ready to lead.

Enough!

It can be a little tedious for rabbits with brains to speak to bears who have none. Still, an old friend is an old friend.

In Charge

One of Rabbit's gifts is telling everyone just what to do. His detailed plans require a great deal of explaining, but they do not always work out exactly as he'd hoped.

Did you know?

Rabbit grows orange pumpkins in his garden—but pumpkins can also be red, green, white, or even blue.

pan (helmet)

"Oh, there is so much to do!"

prize-winning carrot

Very Important Rabbit

Rabbit takes care of his garden and protects his vegetables from crows. He also wards off newcomers to the Wood, although his pals are always welcome.

Garden tips:

Frighten away birds and pests any way you can. Scarecrows are particularly good.

Give a firm tug to pull up a tasty carrot treat fresh from the ground.

Pumpkins, carrots, and cabbages need water, sunlight, and soil to grow.

foot taps when anxious

Eeyore's New Tail Contest

When it comes to a tail, either it is there or it isn't—and on one especially gloomy day for Eeyore, his tail definitely is not. Can Eeyore's friends from the Hundred-Acre Wood help him find a new one?

Exhibit A
Christopher Robin thinks a little imagination will solve this problem. It would also help if Eeyore turned around to show everyone what is missing!

EX iBiTA

evidence of a tragedy

Ready and Willing

When a friend is in need, the animals in the Hundred-Acre Wood are only too happy to help. And Eeyore is only too gloomy to be helped.

A Sad Day

Eeyore does a fine job of showing what it is like to lose one's tail: tragic. He is not surprised by the fact that his tail is missing, however. It accounts for a good deal.

CONTEST FOR EEYORE'S TAEL

Sign Up!

Calling all entries! Any friend can join the search for Eeyore's tail.

Honey Prize

Christopher Robin announces that whoever finds the best new tail for Eeyore gets a delicious prize: a pot of honey! What a sweet reward!

······· Piglet's seat

Eeyore's Many Tails

When a donkey needs a tail, not just anything will do. Eeyore's friends search far and wide for the best new "tail" they can find, but nothing seems quite up to the job.

Accordion tail

good: musical

bad: noisy

Moose head tail

good: two heads are better than one!

bad: too big

Pooh-koo clock tail

good: punctual

bad: breakable

Weather vane tail

good: informative

bad: attractive to lightning

Yo-yo tail

good: playful

bad: rather hard on the head

Scarf tail

good: cozy

bad: unravels easily

B'loon Tail

With its cheerful color, B'loon seems to be the perfect tail for Eeyore, but Eeyore gets a little carried away!

Umbrella tail

good: stops the rain

bad: catches the wind

Party hat tail

good: festive

bad: too silly

The Backson

.... crayon

It is the most fearsome, ferocious, greedy monster you can think of—it's the Backson! Hold onto your socks, this busy bad guy is on the loose.

Taking Note
Pooh is *so* close to a yummy snack when Owl spies the note he is holding.

GON OUT BIZY BACK SOON C.R.

Spell it Out
Owl can read most things, but the tricky words in Christopher Robin's note look especially mysterious.

blue fur
....

Scary sketches:

If the animals' drawings are to be believed, the Backson looks as scary as he sounds. He has pointy horns, big claws, and a giant body.

chalkboard   the Backson breaks crayons

the Backson tangles up ornaments

undamaged sock

Quick on the Draw

Who scribbled all those marks in the library books? Shhhhhh—it was the horrible Backson!

Cold Feet

Feel a draft on your big toe? Maybe it's getting cold round here—or maybe the Backson poked a hole in your sock!

Fearsome Fiend

The Backson is all the worst things you could imagine rolled into one. In fact, the scariest monster is an imaginary one!

Stopped clocks

No wonder the animals are often late! The nasty old Backson has been stopping all of their clocks.

Did you know?

Some donkeys have stripes across their shoulders. Eeyore doesn't—until Tigger gets his paws on him, that is. Then he has them all over!

Add a Little Bounce

A spring on Eeyore's backside helps him to soar as high as bouncy Tigger.

Earn your Stripes

A Tigger is ever so proud of his stripes, so naturally Tigger II should have some, too!

Full of Beans

Eeyore is not excited to be "Tiggerized," but it is hard to discourage a friend who is as bouncy and pouncy as Tigger.

pumpkin mouthpiece to protect teeth

Knockout!
With boxing gloves on his paws, Eeyore gets into shape. But the Tigger spirit just does not come naturally to him.

boxing bell

Tiggerizing Eeyore

The most wonderful thing about Tiggers is that there is only one—or is there? When Tigger tries to turn Eeyore into Tigger II, his makeover creates... the same old Eeyore!

Pooh's Honey Dream

What are a Pooh Bear's dreams made of? Honey, of course! His tummy rumbles about it all the time, and sometimes Pooh gets to daydreaming....

Honey Hungry

Pooh and his tummy have been looking for honey for so long that he starts to dream about it.

Sweet Sands

In Pooh's dream, even the beach is made of honey. What could be sweeter than honey between your toes?

Pooh's beach outfit

Under the Sea

In the honey sea, the fish look like honeybees, there are honeypot crabs, and coral reefs are made out of delicious honeycomb!

honey
palm tree

Honey everywhere:

Pooh is dressed in bee stripes and is ready to go diving in tasty, ooey gooey honey.

pot lid

bee
swimsuit

Winnie the Pooh is so hungry that his friends start to look like honeypots!

A Real Honey Bear
Dream Pooh was enjoying oodles of honey, but real Pooh wakes up to discover he has been eating mud instead of honey. Oh bother!

sticky
licky pot

The Backson Trap

picnic basket

How do you stop something as scary as a Backson? It takes a clever plan, tempting bait, and a lot of good friends. It is time to dig a Backson Trap!

First, Dig a Hole
Work as a team and digging will go twice as fast. Or just get Piglet to do all the hard work.

Anchor Antics
Eeyore's new anchor tail seems just the thing to pull Pooh from the Backson Trap, but it pulls them all toward the trap instead!

Disguise the trap...
A picnic blanket makes a good cover-up. What Backson would not like a sunny picnic lunch?

...with tasty bait
Just remember the important rule of a Backson Trap: Don't fall in it—no matter how yummy the bait looks.

A tempting trail:

The Backson likes destroying anything and everything, so a trail of toys, books, and food is a clever way of getting the Backson near the trap.

Helping Hands

When Pooh and his pals end up in the trap, things look bad. Piglet might be scared, but he is the only one who can help.

Eeyore's anchor tail

It Works!

A trial run can prove the trap is working. However, Pooh discovers it would be safer to wait and watch from above!

upside-down Piglet

teacup helmet

daisy (perennial)

Brave Piglet

Piglet stays above the trap to offer helpful—and not so helpful—tools for pulling his friends to safety.

Caught in the Trap

There's only one problem with a Backson trap: finding a way out of it! The friends are stuck in the trap and only valiant little Piglet can help them now.

long book

"Long Enough?"

A daisy is not long enough to pull Piglet's friends from the trap, but this storybook is the longest thing Piglet ever heard!

... Piglet's bow

Snip, Snip, Snip
A long rope is perfect for climbing out of a Backson trap with. Six short ropes are not, but Piglet can make a pretty bow with them.

scissors .....

The Stuck Six
It can be hard to stay cheerful when one's fate rests on a very small pig. A book landing on poor Pooh's head cannot help.

Up in the Air
In the shadows of the dark and twisty trees, everything looks spookier—even Piglet's trusty red buddy B'loon!

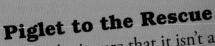

Piglet to the Rescue
When he is sure that it isn't a monster in the branches, Piglet is more than happy to help his friend get unstuck.

Piglet's Scary Adventure

Through a dark Wood travels a little pig in search of a jump rope to help his friends out of a trap. Can Piglet make it to Christopher Robin's house all by himself?

fists held tight

Piglet's armor:

cup

A Very Small Animal feels bolder with the right armor.

spoon

Piglet favors a teacup helmet and a saucer shield to protect him from the Backson.

saucer

A teaspoon is a handy weapon should the Backson get too close to Piglet.

honeypot on Tigger's hand

leaves and branches

Backson Tigger
In his Backson-hunting disguise, Tigger looks just as scary as the Backson himself!

pumpkin on foot

Scared Piglet
Piglet is frightened to face the forest alone, but he bravely continues on to try to help his friends.

Hmmmmm...
Owl's new bellpull looks familiar... Suddenly, Pooh realizes where he has seen it before: on Eeyore's backside!

pink bow

Pinning the Tail on the Donkey

The animals eventually escape the trap and find Christopher Robin safe and well. They are relieved to find out that the "Backson" was all just a silly misunderstanding. Even Eeyore is as happy as he gets. He has a new (old) tail… and with a bright pink bow, to boot!

Hooray for Pooh Bear!

As a reward for finding Eeyore's lost tail, Pooh wins a cheer from his friends and an enormous pot of honey, which he promptly dives right in to.

the grand prize

DK | Penguin Random House

Project Editor Victoria Taylor
Editor Hannah Dolan
Senior Designer Lynne Moulding
Designer Thelma-Jane Robb
Pre-Production Producer Siu Yin Chan
Senior Producer Mary Slater
Managing Editor Sadie Smith
Managing Art Editors Guy Harvey,
Vicky Short, Ron Stobbart
Creative Manager Sarah Harland
Publisher Julie Ferris
Art Director Lisa Lanzarini
Publishing Director Simon Beecroft

First American Edition, 2011
Published in the United States by DK Publishing
1450 Broadway, Suite 801, New York, New York 10018
DK, a Division of Penguin Random House LLC

19 20 21 22 10 9 8 7 6 5 4 3 2
008—176619—June/11

Page design copyright ©2019 Dorling Kindersley Limited

The publisher would like to thank Laura Gilbert for her editorial
assistance; Chelsea Alon, Lauren Kressel, Elaine Lopez-Levine, Nancy
Parent, and Shiho Tilley at Disney Publishing; Renato Lattanzi at Disney
Consumer Products; Jenny Bettis and Peter Del Vecho at Walt Disney
Animation Studios.

www.dk.com

A WORLD OF IDEAS:
SEE ALL THERE IS TO KNOW